Christmas Mice!

Christmas Mice!

by Bethany Roberts

illustrated by Doug Cushman

SCHOLASTIC INC.

New York Toronto London Auckland Sydney
Mexico City New Delhi Hong Kong Buenos Aires

ISBN 0-439-28908-4

12 11 10 9 8 7 6 5 4 3 2 1   1 2 3 4 5 6/0

Printed in the U.S.A.   24

First Scholastic printing, November 2001

The illustrations for this book were executed in watercolor.
The text was set in 24-point Stone Serif.

Christmas mice
deck the house.

Wreath the door.
Pound, pound, pound!

Christmas mice
wrap lots of presents.

Shiny ribbons,
round and round!

Christmas mice
trim the tree.

Put a star
on the top, top, top!

Christmas mice
bake yummy goodies.

Flour everywhere.
Mop, mop, mop!

Christmas secrets.
Stop! Don't peek!

Now out in the snow
to sing, sing, sing!

Merry, merry!
Joy, joy, joy!

Jingle bells!
Ring, ring, ring!

Across the sky—
a spot, a streak.

"Peace to all!"
Did you hear that?

 Look—a paw print
in the snow.

Someone's been here!
Yikes! The cat!

What's this? A gift!
"From Cat to Mice."

A Christmas cheese!
Oh, yum, yum, yum!

The cat has caught
our Christmas cheer!

Now let's thank
our new-found chum.

Wrap one last gift—
"From Mice to Cat."

Tie it with
a big red bow.

Leave it here,
right by her door.

"Merry Christmas—

"Ho, ho, ho!"